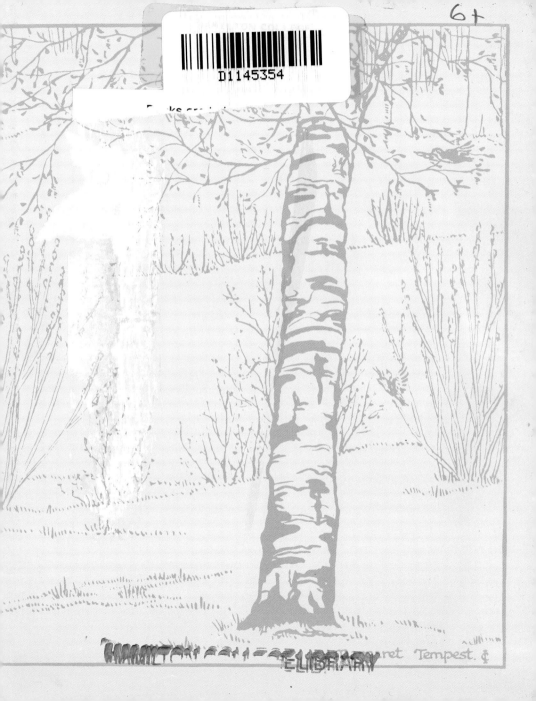

6t

Margaret Tempest.

Hare and the Easter Eggs was first published
in Great Britain by William Collins Sons & Co 1952

This edition published by HarperCollins*Publishers* 2000
Abridged text copyright © The Alison Uttley Literary Property Trust 2000
Illustrations copyright © The Estate of Margaret Tempest 2000
Copyright this arrangement © HarperCollins*Publishers* 2000
Additional illustration by Mark Burgess
Little Grey Rabbit ® and the Little Grey Rabbit logo are
trademarks of HarperCollins*Publishers* Limited

1 3 5 7 9 10 8 6 4 2

ISBN: 000 198396-2

The HarperCollins website address is: www.**fire**and**water**.com

Printed and bound in Singapore

HARE AND THE EASTER EGGS

ALISON UTTLEY

Pictures by Margaret Tempest

Collins

An Imprint of HarperCollins*Publishers*

ONE EVENING in Spring, Hare was dancing along the fields, skipping and tripping and bowing to the rabbits. It was the month of March and he was feeling excited and wild, for all hares are mad in March.

"I'll go to the village," said he. "I'll go and see what there is to be seen and tell them at home all about it. I feel very brave tonight."

He stuck a primrose in his coat for luck and a cowslip in his collar for bravery, and he cut a hazel switch with catkins dangling from it, just in case.

"I'll look at the village shop and see if Mrs Bunting and the shop-bell are still there."

It was dusk when he reached the village and the children were indoors having tea. Not even a dog or cat was to be seen. Hare leapt softly and swiftly down the cobbled street.

He gave a chirrup of joy when he saw that the shop was still open. Jars of sweets in the window shone with many colours in the light of the lamp.

Hare crept close. It was a lovely sight! Whips and tops, dolls and toy horses, cakes and buns were there.

Then he opened his eyes very wide, for he saw something strange. On a dish lay a pile of chocolate eggs with sugary flowers and 'Happy Easter' written on them. Ribbons were tied round them in blue, pink and yellow bows.

"Eggs! 'Normous eggs!"
whispered Hare.

He stared and licked his lips.
"What kind of hen lays these
pretty eggs? I should like to take
Grey Rabbit one, and Squirrel
one and me one."

He pressed closer to the glass and his long ears
flapped against the pane. Just then footsteps came
down the street, and he slipped into the shadows
and crouched there dark as night. His fur quivered,
and his heart thumped.

A woman stopped at the shop window, so close
to Hare that her skirt brushed his ears. She lifted
the door latch and pushed open the door. A loud
tinkle-tinkle came from the bell hanging above it.

"The bell's telling who comes into the shop,"
thought Hare.

"Good evening, Mrs Bunting," called the
woman. "Those are nice Easter eggs. How much
are they?"

"A shilling each, Mrs Snowball," replied Mrs
Bunting, and she set the dish on the counter.

Hare crept into the shop and stood by Mrs
Snowball's skirts with his nose raised, sniffing
the sweet smells of chocolate and new bread.

Mrs Snowball chose her egg and as the two women chatted, Hare stretched out a furry paw, took a leap, and snatched a chocolate egg. In a moment he was gone, out into the dusk.

"Oh! Oh!" cried Mrs Bunting. "What was that? Something took an egg!"

"I didn't see anything," said Mrs Snowball.

They both ran to the shop door, but Hare was already far away, running like the wind.

"You can't catch me," he laughed. He stopped to look at the egg. His warm fur had softened the chocolate and his fist went through. He brought out a little fluffy chicken made of silk and wool.

Hare licked his paws and then licked the egg.

"Oh! De-larcious!" he cried, and soon the egg disappeared.

"That's the best egg I've ever tasted," said he, and he galloped across the common and dashed into the little house where Grey Rabbit was cooking the supper.

"Here you come at last, Hare," cried Squirrel. "What have you been eating? You are brown and dirty."

"Not dirt, Squirrel, it's chocolate," panted Hare. "You'll never guess! I've eaten an egg laid by an Easter hen and it was made of chocolate," he said proudly.

"Nonsense," snapped Squirrel.

"Chocolate egg?" cried Grey Rabbit. "Where was it?"

"In the village shop," said Hare. "I took it right under the nose of Mrs Bunting. I shall go and pay for it," explained Hare. "It was a shilling."

"You took an egg and you ate it all yourself," said Squirrel. "Greedy Hare!"

"I brought you the ribbon, Squirrel, and the little fluffy chicken inside the egg is for Grey Rabbit," said Hare.

All evening they talked of Easter eggs.

16

The next morning, after breakfast, the three set off for Wise Owl's house. They couldn't wait till night, so they had to wake the Owl from his sleep. They rang the little silver bell and they stood in a row under the tree waiting for him.

"Who's there?" hooted Wise Owl very crossly. "Go away or I'll eat you."

"Please, Wise Owl..." began Grey Rabbit, waving her handkerchief for a truce.

"We want to know..." added Squirrel, stammering with fright.

"About Easter Eggs," shouted Hare in a loud voice. "Chocolate ones."

"And who lays them," whispered Grey Rabbit.

"I've got a good mind to tell you nothing," said Wise Owl, frowning at the noisy Hare. "But remembering the primrose wine, and thinking of eggs you will bring me, I'll speak."

"Yes, Wise Owl," said Grey Rabbit meekly. "Hoots and toots," snorted Hare.

"Easter eggs come at Easter, for children and good Rabbits but not for Hares," said Wise Owl.

"The church bells ring, and the little birds sing, and the sun dances on Easter morning."

He blinked and yawned and went to bed, banging his door so that the bough shook.

Grey Rabbit and Squirrel went home, but Hare leapt aside and ran across the fields. He tapped on Mole's door.

"Moldy Warp? Quick! Are you at home?" he called.

"What's the hurry, Hare?" asked the Mole.

"Can you lend me a silver penny, or a gold penny or anything?" Hare asked.

"What's it for, Hare?"

"For a secret, a fine secret. I owe a silver penny and if you could give me an extra one…" said Hare.

Moldy Warp went into his underground house and brought up a fistful of gold coins.

"You can have these if you'll do something for me," said he.

"Oh, thank you, Moldy Warp. You are a real friend," cried Hare stuffing the coins in his pocket.

"I have a fancy for some eggs," said Moldy Warp.

"I'll bring you some at once," said Hare, gladly. "I'll go to old Speckeldy Hen."

21

Speckledy Hen was in the meadow, scratching among the daisies when Hare came up.

"Please, Speckledy Hen, can I have some eggs for Moldy Warp?" asked Hare.

"I wanted to give Grey Rabbit my eggs," said the Hen. "Why should I send them to the Mole?"

"He wants them very special," said Hare. "Do please let me have them, Speckledy Hen."

"Very well. As it's nearly Easter, I will," said the Hen. She filled a basket from the store of eggs in the barn.

"These have been laid by my friends, but my own egg is for Grey Rabbit."

Hare carried the eggs to Mole.

"I'm going to be very busy," said Moldy Warp. "I'm getting ready for Easter." He carried the eggs indoors and shut the door.

"I've got a secret, a secret, a secret," sang Hare, leaping towards home.

When he got to the little house he kept jingling the coins in his pocket.

"What makes that jingle-jangle in your pocket, Hare?" asked Squirrel.

"It's a secret," said Hare. He took out his watch and shook it and altered the fingers to make the time pass more quickly.

"I'm going out again tonight," he announced.

"You'll take care, won't you?" asked Grey Rabbit.

As soon as tea was over he went to the village, for he wanted another look at the Easter eggs.

Hare had some difficulty in getting to the shop, for children were looking in at the window. He had to wait until they went away, and when all was safe he darted across the road.

"I'll wait till somebody comes along and Mrs Bunting opens the door."

Hare leaned against the door, but it was not fastened, and his fat little body fell inside the shop.

"Tinkle! Tinkle! Tinkle!" rang the little bell.

"Oh dear!" cried Hare.

Mrs Bunting heard the jingling bell, but she stopped to take the kettle off the fire in the back room. That gave Hare his chance. He dived into a brown jug which stood near.

"Drat those children! They're after my Easter eggs," said Mrs Bunting. "Well, it's time to shut up shop."

She locked and bolted the door. She took the money from the till and turned down the lamp. Then she went to the back room and shut the door.

Hare stood on his head in the jug. He heard the sounds of door and shutters, but he was too busy trying not to sneeze to bother about them.

Slowly he pushed up his long ears, his round head and his astonished eyes. There, watching him, sat a fine tabby cat. The two stared hard at each other.

"Good evening," said Hare, and he scrambled out and made a deep bow.

"Gracious me!" exclaimed the Tabby. "Pleased to meet you, Mister Hare."

"At your service, ma'am," said Hare politely.

"What are you doing here? It isn't safe," said the Cat.

"I'm here to pay a debt," said Hare.

"Hist!" cried the Cat, and Hare leapt back in the jug as the door opened and Mrs Bunting appeared.

29

"Come along Puss," she said.

"Miaow! Miaow!" cried the Cat, retreating to a corner.

"Oh, very well! Perhaps there's a mouse," said Mrs Bunting. She fetched a saucerful of milk and shut the door.

"You can come out now," whispered the Cat. "She'll go to bed soon."

Hare climbed out clutching the gold coins.

"I've come to buy some Easter eggs," said he. "Here's the money."

"This will buy up the shop," said the Cat. "We never see any gold, only shillings and pennies."

Mrs Bunting's footsteps thudded up the stairs into the bedroom over the shop.

"Now we can talk," said the Cat with relief.
"I want to hear about you and Squirrel and Grey
Rabbit. I'll get you a bite to eat first."

She fetched some sausages and ham from the
counter and sugary buns from the window.

"Eat these, Hare," said she, and Hare gobbled them up.

He told all his adventures and many more, and the Cat thought he was the bravest, boldest animal she had ever met.

The evening wore on, the moon peered through a chink in the shutters and smiled at the sight of these two together.

Wise Owl came hooting over the roof, and Hare told about him. The Fox came snuffling outside and Hare told about him too. The Weasels squeaked as they ran down the street and Hare told of them and their tricks.

Then his head nodded, and he slept.

Dawn came with the crowing of cocks and Hare opened his eyes.

"It's time you were off, Hare," said the Cat. "I'll open the door for you."

Hare packed the Easter eggs in a basket while the Cat unlocked the door. She wrapped a duster round the chattering tongue of the little bell and opened the door.

Hare poured his gold coins on the dish, and seized the basket of eggs.

"Goodbye, Mistress Tabby," said he. "Thank you very much for your kindness."

"Miaow! Miaow!" answered the Cat.

Hare didn't wait any longer.

Hare hid the chocolate eggs in the empty beehive, and then he crept into bed.

"Would you like an Easter egg party?" asked Grey Rabbit after breakfast the next morning. "We will invite our dear friends to see the sun dance on Easter morning."

"Oh yes," cried Squirrel.

So Grey Rabbit made a heap of tiny cakes, each in the shape of a moon. Squirrel and Hare scribbled the invitations on primrose petals. Squirrel was a poor writer and Hare couldn't spell, so they put the letter E and nothing else.

Squirrel had knitted an egg for Grey Rabbit. She made it of blue wool and she stuffed it with nuts.

On Easter morning Grey Rabbit, Squirrel and Hare went to the garden in the early light. Hare was very excited about something. Grey Rabbit wondered why he kept looking at the beehive.

"We haven't any bees, Hare," she reminded him.

Footsteps came pattering down the lane and little voices could be heard singing songs.

"We didn't invite all these," whispered Squirrel.

"Please, Grey Rabbit, we've come to wish you a Happy Easter," said the small creatures of the woodland in shrill chorus. "A Happy Easter."

"A Happy Easter," replied Grey Rabbit.

Away in the east the sky was bathed in golden light, and rosy clouds floated above the rising sun.

All the animals gazed into the sky, and they saw the great ball of the sun come up from behind the hills, and dance that Easter morning.

Then Moldy Warp brought his basket of coloured eggs.

"These are magical eggs," said Grey Rabbit. "How ever did you make them, Moldy Warp?"

Rat came forward with a little bone egg which opened. Grey Rabbit opened it and found a wooden thimble and a few thorn pins.

"How clever of you to carve this little Easter egg!" said Grey Rabbit.

Squirrel offered her queer knitted egg, crooked and fat, and Grey Rabbit hugged her friend.

Next, old Hedgehog and Fuzzypeg came with duck eggs, and the Speckledy Hen brought her own new-laid egg.

All this time Hare had been dodging backwards and forwards, glancing at the beehive, and then going away. At last he lifted the straw skep and brought out the chocolate eggs.

"Grey Rabbit, Squirrel, Hedgehog family, Speckledy Hen, Moldy Warp, and all, I wish you a Happy Easter," said he.

On the grass he spread the chocolate eggs with their bright ribbons and curly lettering, and everybody cried out in surprise and pleasure.

Wise Owl, flying over, dived down and seized an egg. He pierced it with his beak and brought out the fluffy toy chick.

"Bah! A trick!" he snorted, and away he flew.

Hare mopped his forehead.

"Where did these come from?" Grey Rabbit asked.

"I bought them," said Hare. "Moldy Warp gave me the money. They are from Moldy Warp and me."

Moldy Warp looked surprised, and he stroked one of the eggs.

"Soft as velvet, sweet as honey," said he. "Bought with Roman gold, these eggs."

They sat on the ground in a circle and drank tiny glasses of primrose wine and ate bits of the Eater eggs.

"A Happy Easter," they said to one another, holding high their glasses.

Hare told his adventure, and they all thought he was a very clever Hare.

"Of course I am," said Hare. "I've been telling you for years, but you wouldn't believe me."